Mr. Putter & Tabby
Spin the Yarn

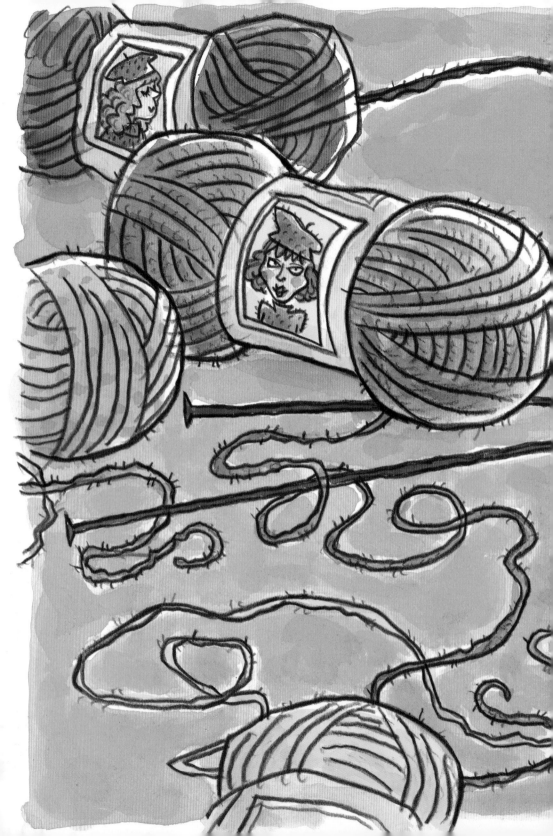

CYNTHIA RYLANT

Mr. Putter & Tabby
Spin the Yarn

Illustrated by

ARTHUR HOWARD

Harcourt, Inc.
Orlando Austin New York San Diego Toronto London

For Cheryl Harshman
—C. R.

Text copyright © 2006 by Cynthia Rylant
Illustrations copyright © 2006 by Arthur Howard

www.HarcourtBooks.com

Library of Congress Cataloging-in-Publication Data
Rylant, Cynthia.
Mr. Putter & Tabby spin the yarn/Cynthia Rylant; illustrated by Arthur Howard.
p. cm.
Summary: Trying to be neighborly, Mr. Putter decides to serve tea to
Mrs. Teaberry's knitting club but chaos ensues when Tabby the cat and
Zeke the dog find the party irresistible.
[1. Neighborliness—Fiction. 2. Cats—Fiction. 3. Dogs—Fiction.]
I. Title: Mr. Putter and Tabby spin the yarn. II. Howard, Arthur, ill. III. Title.
PZ7.R982Muc 2006
[E]—dc22   2005024761
ISBN-13: 978-0-15-205067-2   ISBN-10: 0-15-205067-1

Manufactured in China

First edition

A C E G H F D B

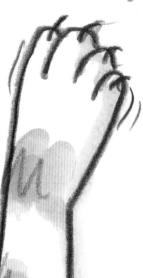

1

Good Neighbors

Mr. Putter and his fine cat, Tabby,
lived next door to Mrs. Teaberry
and her good dog, Zeke.
Mr. Putter liked Mrs. Teaberry.
She was a good neighbor.

She made chocolate crunchies
and shared them with him.

She made raspberry roll-ups and
shared those.

She made brown sugar bonbons
and shared those, too.
She was a *very* good neighbor.

Sometimes Mr. Putter
was not sure if *he*
was a good neighbor.
All he did was eat Mrs. Teaberry's food.

"All I do is eat Mrs. Teaberry's food,"
Mr. Putter told Tabby one day.
"I should do something nice for her."

It happened that Mrs. Teaberry
and Zeke stopped by later that day.
They had just returned
from the yarn shop.
"I am starting a knitting club,"
said Mrs. Teaberry.
"We are going to meet at my house and knit."
"How nice!" said Mr. Putter.
"Would you like to join?" asked Mrs. Teaberry.

"No, thank you," said Mr. Putter, removing a shoe from Zeke's mouth.

Suddenly Mr. Putter had an idea.

"Why don't I serve tea to your club?" he said.

"You can knit and I can pour."

"How nice!" said Mrs. Teaberry.

"Can you stop in tomorrow at two?" she asked.

"Will do!" said Mr. Putter, removing a glove
from Zeke's mouth.

Mrs. Teaberry and Zeke went home.

Mr. Putter looked at Tabby.

"We are going to be good neighbors," he said.

Tabby purred and purred.

2
The Club

The next day at two, Mr. Putter and Tabby went next door to Mrs. Teaberry's house.

There were a lot of ladies there.
They were knitting madly
and talking loudly.

Tabby looked at all the needles
and all the threads and all the
big balls of yarn.
Her teeth began to chatter.
Chat-chat-chat went Tabby's teeth.
(This sometimes happened when
Tabby was excited.)

She looked at the big balls of yarn
spinning.
Chat-chat-chat.

Mr. Putter petted her to calm her down.
But there were about fifty pounds
of yarn in the room.
Petting wasn't helping.

Everyone said a cheery hello
to Mr. Putter and Tabby.
"Where's Zeke?" asked Mr. Putter.
"I closed him in the kitchen,"
said Mrs. Teaberry.
"He was bothering Gertrude's hat."

Gertrude was wearing a hat
with lots of fake vegetables on it.
"He kept stealing the potatoes,"
said Mrs. Teaberry.

"Tabby and I shall keep him company,"
said Mr. Putter.

"Thank you!" said Mrs. Teaberry.

"You are a good neighbor!"

That is just what Mr. Putter
wanted to hear.

3
The Fun Starts

In the kitchen Zeke had found
a bag of popcorn, a loaf of bread,
and some marshmallows.
He also had a fake potato.
"Oh dear," said Mr. Putter.

He cleaned up the mess.
He helped Zeke unstick
a marshmallow from his teeth.

Then Mr. Putter made tea.
He fixed a nice big tray with
a teapot and tea cozy.
He put sugar cubes and cream
on the tray.
And he filled a big bowl
with chocolate bridge mix.

Zeke and Tabby were very interested.

"Hmmm," said Mr. Putter.

He poured some cream in a bowl

for them to share.

Tabby purred and Zeke wagged.

It was time to serve tea.

"If you're a good dog, Zeke,"
said Mr. Putter, "you can help."
Zeke wagged again.
Mr. Putter opened the kitchen door.
And that's when the fun started.

4
One Less Potato

Zeke went straight for the hat.

"Eeek!" screamed Gertrude.

Zeke flew through the house with a big
plastic potato in his mouth.

Tabby chattered herself into a frenzy.
Then she went straight for the nearest
ball of yarn (which happened to be
connected to a sweater
Mrs. Fitzwater had been knitting
for seven months).

Tabby flew through the house with
the yarn in her mouth.

As Mr. Putter stood in the doorway
with his lovely tray of tea,
Mrs. Fitzwater's sweater got smaller
and smaller
and smaller.

Then it disappeared.

When the excitement was over,
Tabby and Zeke were long gone,
and the room had one less potato
and no sweater.

Mr. Putter looked at the knitting club.

He put on his best smile.

"One lump or two, ladies?"

he asked.

At first Gertrude and Mrs. Fitzwater
were too grumpy for tea.
But Mr. Putter charmed them.

He told Gertrude she had perfect
taste in hats.

He told Mrs. Fitzwater she was
a model of goodness to cats.

He gave them extra bridge mix.
He poured them lots of tea.
Mrs. Teaberry stopped saying, "Oh dear."
And the knitting club had a wonderful
visit with Mr. Putter.

By the time the tea was over,
Gertrude had promised to make Mr. Putter
his own vegetable hat,
and Mrs. Fitzwater had promised him
a sweater.

When Tabby and Zeke finally came back
(looking as if someone had knitted *them*),
everyone just laughed.

Mrs. Teaberry was so happy.
When the knitting club went home,
she thanked Mr. Putter.
"You saved the day," she said.
"Yes," said Mr. Putter. "But now I
have to wear a vegetable hat."

"Oh, don't worry," said Mrs. Teaberry.
"Zeke will take care of that!"

The illustrations in this book were done in pencil,
watercolor, and gouache on 250-gram cotton rag paper.
The display type was set in Artcraft.
The text type was set in Berkeley Old Style Book.
Color separations by Bright Arts Ltd., Hong Kong
Manufactured by South China Printing Company, Ltd., China
This book was printed on totally chlorine-free Stora Enso Matte paper.
Production supervision by Pascha Gerlinger
Designed by Arthur Howard and Lauren Rille